The Dream Jar

by Bonnie Pryor

illustrated by Mark Graham

Morrow Junior Books · New York

To Tonya, for knowing that hard work makes dreams come true

—B.P.

To Dasha

—M.G.

Oil paints were used for the full-color illustrations.
The text type is 16-point Weiss.

Printed in Hong Kong by South China Printing Company (1988) Ltd.

1 2 3 4 5 6 7 8 9 10

Library of Congress Cataloging-in-Publication Data
Pryor, Bonnie.
The dream jar/by Bonnie Pryor; illustrated by Mark Graham.
p. cm.
Summary: After emigrating to America, each member of a Russian family works hard to contribute to the family's dream of someday owning and running a store.
ISBN 0-688-13061-5 (trade)—ISBN 0-688-13062-3 (library)
[1. Emigration and immigration—Fiction. 2. Family life—Fiction. 3. Russian Americans—Fiction.] I. Graham, Mark, ill. II. Title. PZ7.P94965Dr 1996
[E]—dc20 95-13710 CIP AC

Valentina loved to hear her papa sing. Each morning in Russia, before she opened her eyes, she had listened for his song. On good days, Papa sang silly songs that made her bounce out of bed with a giggle. On other days he sang so softly Valentina thought of the winter wind sighing through the trees.

In Russia, Papa had been a farmer. "Come here, my little Valechka," he would say, lifting her into the wagon piled high with cabbages and beets. Valentina remembered the smell of the horses as they rode to the city. But most of all she remembered Papa's songs.

Since they had come to America, Papa did not sing at all. From morning's light until dark he worked laying brick to make buildings. After supper he was so tired he fell asleep in his chair.

"Sing for us, Papa," Valentina and her brother, Michael, would beg.

"Maybe tomorrow," Papa always answered.

One Sunday Valentina was looking out the tiny window to the dirty street below. "It's too dark and noisy here," she complained to her mother. "That's why Papa doesn't sing."

The good smell of meat and onions filled the tiny kitchen as Mama stuffed the dough to make *pelmini* for dinner. "Someday we will have a house of our own," she said, "and Papa will have a store where fine ladies come to shop. Then Papa will sing again."

"What will we sell in our store?" Valentina asked.

"Everything," exclaimed Papa. "Everything in one store! What a convenience—people won't have to go to the baker and the butcher or the fish vendors anymore. And we will have the freshest vegetables and the tastiest breads...."

"But first," said Mama, "we must save enough money to buy the store."

"I can help," said Valentina.

"You are too little, Valechka," Papa said. "You must go to school and learn how to be a real American girl."

Every Sunday Mama put the few coins she'd managed to save into a big jar. "This is for our dream," she said.

"The baker gave me ten cents for sweeping out the store," Michael bragged as he added a coin to the jar. "And he said if I come every morning before school and deliver bread and rolls, he will give me three dollars every week."

Valentina glared at her brother. "Michael is such a show-off," she said, stamping her foot. "I want to work and put money in the jar too."

Mama frowned. "Don't disturb Mrs. Sarbiewski downstairs," she said. "You are too little to work." Even though Mama kissed her cheek, Valentina didn't smile.

Every morning, while it was still dark, Valentina hurried to fill a bucket of water from the pipe in the hall. While the water was boiling for coffee, Mama sliced bread and cheese for breakfast and packed Papa's lunch in a bucket.

Mama and Aunt Katherine earned money through piecework, sewing parts of clothing. As soon as the first streaks of light shone through the grimy window, they began. Mama's head was bent over the tiny stitches, and her hands were black from the dye. But Valentina knew if her mama sewed all day she could make five dollars a week, with a little extra for the dream.

Valentina was thinking about Papa's wonderful idea while she did the dishes and watched the babies until it was time for school. Everything in one store! If only she could do something to help. Then she ran down the three flights of stairs to the street below.

EAST SIDE
ICE

The ice wagon rumbled to a stop at the next tenement. Valentina had to shout to be heard over the noise of the street. "Do you need any help?"

The iceman laughed. "What could you do, little one? These blocks are much too heavy."

Valentina pushed past vendors selling wares from their little carts. "Needles and pins!" shouted one. "Fresh fish!" shouted another. But it was the same whenever she asked. No one needed any help from a small girl.

Even though her teacher never smiled, Valentina liked school. Michael sat on the boys' side of the room. Valentina sat with the other girls and carefully copied her lessons. The bigger boys laughed when she made mistakes, but Valentina pretended not to hear. One day Michael fell asleep and Miss Braun rapped his knuckles with a stick. When the other boys laughed, Valentina made a face and stuck out her tongue. But she was careful not to let Miss Braun see.

After that day Michael did not go back to school. "I'm going to work all morning for the baker," he told Valentina. "And in the afternoon I will shine shoes. Then I will earn lots of money for the dream."

Mama's smile was sad. "In America I wanted my children to go to school," she said.

"I could teach him, Mama," Valentina offered.

"You're just a baby," Michael scoffed. "I'm too big for you to teach."

"Valentina is not too little to teach me," said Papa.

Now Valentina studied even harder. And every night after supper she taught Michael and Papa everything she had learned that day in school. Mama listened as she sewed.

But Valentina still was not happy. "Why can't I help earn money for the dream?" she complained one day to Papa. "I want to help too."

"You do help," Papa answered. "Your job is to watch the babies so Mama can sew. And to teach your brother and papa to read."

But Valentina noticed Michael's proud smirk when he put five whole dollars into the jar the next week. "With my help, Papa will soon have his store," he bragged.

Then winter came and the snow piled up in dirty drifts against the buildings. Some days there was no work for Papa. Mama sewed even longer each day, but still she had to take money out of the dream jar to pay the rent. Every day Papa went out looking for work. And every night he came home looking tired and sad. Valentina sang all the funny songs she could remember, but Papa didn't smile.

One day Mrs. Sarbiewski knocked at the door. "This letter came for me today," she said, looking worried. "But I can't read these American words."

Valentina looked carefully at the letter. "It says a package has arrived for you," she told Mrs. Sarbiewski. "This is the address where you can pick it up."

"You are lucky to have such a smart daughter," Mrs. Sarbiewski told Papa.

"My Valechka is teaching me to read and speak like an American," Papa said proudly, showing Mrs. Sarbiewski his lessons.

"The school has classes at night to help us," said Mrs. Sarbiewski. "But with two babies to tend how can I go?"

Suddenly Valentina had an idea. "You can bring them here," she said. "I'll teach you too."

"That would be wonderful," Mrs. Sarbiewski said happily. "I will give you ten cents a week."

Mrs. Sarbiewski was not the only one who wanted to learn. When she came the next night, she brought Mr. Hromey from next door. Then came Mr. and Mrs. Torkarski from upstairs and Mr. Sincak from the first floor. Everyone crowded around the table in the tiny kitchen. Valentina made them copy each word ten times just like Miss Braun made her do at school.

"No time for gossiping, Mrs. Sarbiewski," she scolded. "Papa, have you learned the names of all the presidents?"

The next Sunday Valentina proudly added one dollar to the dream jar.

Even when the snow melted and Papa went back to work, Valentina kept teaching her school. "I would like to be a real teacher when I grow up," Valentina said one evening.

"You are a real teacher right now," said Mr. Sincak. "Because of you my boss gave me a better job."

That spring and summer Papa worked every day harder than ever. But now he did not fall asleep after supper. Instead, Valentina would hear him talking and laughing with Mama far into the night.

One day Papa counted the money in the jar. Then he swung Valentina around in a circle in his big strong arms and made her laugh. "We have almost enough, Valechka," Papa exclaimed.

Another winter was coming, and the streets were gloomy and dark. But Papa was singing again, so Valentina did not mind. One morning Papa's song was so happy it made Valentina jump right out of bed. "Put on your best dress, Valechka," said Papa. "Today I have a surprise."

Valentina rode on a train that went high above the streets until the crowded buildings and noisy streets were far behind. This part of the city had shops and houses, and even some trees.

"I will show you a great place for shopping," Papa said. He led them to a little store on the corner of a busy street.

Mama shook her head. "What a silly man. I can't go shopping here. It is much too far away from home."

Papa winked at Valentina. "Not if you live right upstairs."

He put his arm around Mama. "This will be our store. It is small now, but someday, if we work hard, it will be the finest store in the city. We will not mind the hard work because behind the store is a little yard and a tree, and upstairs there is a room for Valechka and the babies and another for Michael."

"What about my school?" Valentina said suddenly.

"Don't worry," Papa said. "Mr. Sincak will go to night school. Then he will teach the others."

"And the dream jar?" Valentina asked.

"In America there is room for many dreams. We will keep our dream jar. Then someday you will be a teacher." Papa chuckled. "A teacher with desks for her students instead of a kitchen table."

"Now let's go see our new home," Papa said. Together they climbed up the stairs, singing all the way.